Edward James Watherston

Our Railways: Should They be Private Or National Property?

Antigonos

Edward James Watherston

Our Railways: Should They be Private Or National Property?

Reprint of the original, first published in 1879.

1st Edition 2024 | ISBN: 978-3-38801-046-5

Antigonos Verlag is an imprint of Outlook Verlagsgesellschaft mbH.

Verlag (Publisher): Outlook Verlag GmbH, Zeilweg 44, 60439 Frankfurt, Deutschland, info@outlook-verlag.de
Vertretungsberechtigt (Authorized to represent): E. Roepke, Zeilweg 44, 60439 Frankfurt, Deutschland
Druck (Print): Libri Plureos GmbH, Friedensallee 273, 22763 Hamburg, Deutschland

OUR RAILWAYS:

SHOULD THEY BE

PRIVATE OR NATIONAL PROPERTY?

By EDWARD J. WATHERSTON.

"What we ought to aim at in railways is very much the same as that which was done by the Post Office—that is, to have one rate, if possible, to all places."—G. P. BIDDER, C.E.

LONDON:
EDWARD STANFORD, 55, CHARING CROSS, S.W.

1879.

OUR RAILWAYS.

IT is a fact which I hold to be indisputable that the immense material progress of modern civilization centres around one grand scientific discovery—steam power, chiefly as employed on railways. The men who laid down parallel bars of iron, horizontally, placing the locomotive on them, revolutionized the earth and its inhabitants. It is astounding to think to what an extent this revolution, affecting the deepest interests of mankind, the intercourse between individuals and nations, has developed in the comparatively short time of half a century. The first line of railway served by locomotives, that from Stockton to Darlington, was opened in the autumn of 1825, and at this moment the civilized world is encircled by a network of railways, Europe alone possessing over a hundred thousand miles of iron highroads. No human discovery—not even that wonderful one of the printing press, another revolutionizer of mankind—ever made progress so fast as the modern railway.

Even to the men who originated the railway, and its soul, the locomotive, the progress was amazing. There is no evidence to show that George Stephenson and the friends who helped land, while the total capital of all the Scottish companies is considerably below that of the single London and North-Western Company. While the latter has a paid-up capital of 90,618,108*l.*, the total paid-up capital of all the railways of Scotland amounts to only 87,189,068*l.* The seventeen railway companies existing in North Britain clearly ought to unite; but it is doubtful whether they will do so, any more than the 168 companies of South Britain, unless the Government will take the matter in hand, converting private interests and private property, under the influence of narrow aims—not always even prudently selfish—into national property managed in the national interests.

Of the railways of Ireland little need be said beyond that the leading lines, comparatively short as they are, pay dividends to their shareholders, but that these are obtained only, at the expense of the welfare of the country, by inordinately high rates and fares. The first company, as regards length of lines, the Great Southern and Western of Ireland, which has its seat at Dublin, possesses 486 miles, of which 291 miles are single and 195 miles double, and pays dividends of about 5 per cent. per annum; while the second company, the Great Northern of Ireland, holding 459 miles, of which 323 miles are single and only 136 double lines, has been able, in recent years, to pay between 5½ and 6 per cent. dividends. The third company, the

As to goods in small quantities, they should be treated exactly as letters are by the Post Office, stamps being issued to frank them from one place to any other in the country. The end kept in view in all the reforms thus introduced, the railways being national property, should be to assimilate on the same principle the transport of letters, of telegraphic messages, of persons, and of merchandise. Fully carried out, the system of national railways would bind our population into one compact mass as nothing else could do; it would reduce a thousand irregularities in prices, even of land, and develop prosperity and well-being among the thirty-four millions of the United Kingdom.

LONDON: EDWARD STANFORD, 55, CHARING CROSS, S.W.

him to establish the Stockton and Darlington line—the first railway in the world on which trains were drawn by locomotives—realized at first the stupendous magnitude of the undertaking upon which they were engaged. It is certain that for many years after the opening of the Stockton and Darlington Railway, and its early successor, the Manchester and Liverpool line, the world at large had no faith whatever in the two parallel bars of iron and the steam-propelled trains, that were offered as substitutes for ordinary highroads and coaches drawn by horses. Engineers of the old school sneered at railways; statesmen treated them with contempt; and the municipal authorities of almost every town to which it was proposed to make railways offered the most violent opposition to the schemes submitted to Parliament. The natural result was that in England, the home and mother of railways, their construction was left entirely to private enterprise. It was different in other countries, such as Belgium, where railways grew up at a time when their full importance had come to be appreciated by the leaders of public opinion, the conviction gradually spreading that the new iron lines would be the highroads of the future, and as such ought to be national property. Such an idea never entered the minds of British legislators, who had to pronounce upon the fate of our English railways. Bills for their construction were not only not encouraged, but allowed to pass through Parliament only after terrible procrastination, great opposition, and enormous expense. On many occasions, and by statesmen considered eminent, railways were pronounced a "nuisance"—one noble lord, for some time Prime Minister, asserting that they would be "the curse and the ruin of the country." Had any individual, in either of the Houses of Parliament, proposed to construct railways at the expense and for the benefit of the nation, he would, probably, have been treated as a madman.

It was thus that, against enormous obstacles, railways grew up in this country. George Stephenson and his friends had to fight a Parliamentary battle of no less than three years' duration to get the bills passed for the first trunk railway starting from the Metropolis, that from London to Birmingham, which finally obtained the Royal sanction in May 1833. It was Stephenson's original idea to lay the lines of rails along the course followed by the old highroad connecting the chief towns, but so intense was the public prejudice against the "new-fangled" mode of locomotion, that his plans had to be entirely abandoned, and he was compelled to construct an endless number of tunnels, bridges, and viaducts, in order to keep at a proper distance from the principal centres of population. It was not till after the lapse of another generation that these good towns, which

The earliest "trunk" line

had pronounced railways a " nuisance," if not
"a curse," at last awoke to a sense of their
utility. Then there was a rush in the opposite
direction. There came endless prayers and
petitions that such and such a town, which had
bitterly opposed being on the main line of a
railway, might be favoured with a little branch
line. Many of these now have their small
branches; but they have frequently come to
them only after grass was beginning to grow
in their streets. The mischief thus done was
enormous. Nearly all the trunk lines at first
constructed were badly laid out, and constructed,
besides, at an enormous expense. The railway
from London to Birmingham, which, following
Stephenson's first plan, might have been made
in little more than a year, at an expense of
about a million, or a million and a half, took
five years to construct, and cost over four
millions. It is curious to reflect what an immense saving of money, and, more than this, an
increase of commercial and social gains, might
have been effected if the importance of railways,
now acknowledged by all, had been realized in
this country from the commencement of their
construction.

Growth of our railway system.

That, notwithstanding violent public preju-
dices as well as Parliamentary obstruction,
the growth of the English railway system was
very rapid, was due entirely to the inherent
resources of the country. Even the promoters

of the London and Birmingham line, when they reckoned up the cost of all the tunnels and viaducts which, against reason and common sense, they had been compelled to construct, despaired of the financial success of their undertaking, and before the railway was opened the shares had fallen very low. But a single year's working was sufficient to show that all fears as to the unprofitable character of the enterprise had been unfounded. In spite of its costliness, the line proved a grand commercial success. Then followed, as always in similar instances, a turn of the tide. Men who had sneered before at locomotives and iron highroads now became enthusiastic admirers of them, and railway shares, formerly despised, were fought for. At the end of the year 1825, which saw the opening of the first railway, the line from Stockton to Darlington, the total length of railways in England was 40 miles, and the cost of construction of the same amounted to 120,000*l*., or 3,000*l*. per mile. The increase within the next five years, to the end of 1830, had not risen to more than a total of 95 miles, built at an expenditure of 840,925*l*., the average cost per mile being not more than 8,852*l*., the new lines, constructed during the quinquennial period, consisting chiefly of inexpensive local railways.

With the opening of the first great trunk line, from Manchester to Liverpool, which took place on the 15th of September, 1830—date

made memorable by the killing of the Right
Honourable William Huskisson, under the eyes
of his friend, the Duke of Wellington,—a new
impetus was given to railway enterprise. By
the end of the next quinquennial period,
December 31, 1835, there were 293 miles of
railway, constructed at a cost of 5,648,531*l.*,
being 19,280*l.* per mile on the average. There
was only a doubling of railway mileage in the
first five years after the opening of the Stockton
and Darlington line, while a trebling took place
in the second five-yearly period. In the third,
from 1835 to 1840, while the London and
Birmingham Railway was being constructed
and opened, there was a quintupling of mileage.
At the end of 1840 the total length of railways
in the United Kingdom had risen to 1435 miles,
built at a cost of 41,391,634*l.*, or at an average
of 28,844*l.* per mile. Within the fourth quinquennial period, ending 1845, the growth of the
railways had risen to 2441 miles, and the total
cost to 88,481,371*l.*, the average cost per mile
being 36,247*l.* Finally, during the fifth quinquennial period, up to the end of 1850, com-
pleting the quarter of a century of English railway life, the length of lines rose to 6621 miles,
built at a total expenditure of 240,270,745*l.*,
being at the average rate of 36,290*l.* per mile of
line. It will be seen, from the figures here
given, that the cost of railways per mile increased fourfold from 1830 to 1850. However,

allowance has to be made in this respect for double and single lines. While many of the earlier railways had only single lines, those of later date, connecting great centres of population, had their permanent way made for two or more lines of rails, which, though much enhancing the cost, was undoubtedly the cheapest in the end. At this moment, the double lines in England, by itself, are the rule, and the single lines the exception. In Scotland it is otherwise, however; considerably more than one-half of the railways have only single lines. Again in Ireland, more than three-fourths of the total mileage consists of single lines.

The following table shows, after the last official "Railway Returns" issued by the Board of Trade, the growth of the railway system of the United Kingdom within the last quarter of a century, giving the length of lines, double and more, or single, the total cost of construction, represented by paid-up capital, and the cost per mile of lines open for traffic, in each of the twenty-five years from 1854 to 1878 :—

Growth of railways in a quarter of a century.

Years. December 31st.	Double or more Lines.	Single Lines.	Total.	Total Paid-up Capital.	Cost per Mile of Line open.
	Miles.	Miles.	Miles.	£	£
1854	6103	1950	8,053	286,068,794	35,523
1855	6153	2182	8,335	297,584,709	35,703
1856	6266	2444	8,710	307,595,086	35,315
1857	6357	2682	9,089	315,157,258	34,866
1858	6413	3029	9,542	325,375,507	34,099
1859	6522	3480	10,002	334,362,928	33,430
1860	6690	3743	10,433	348,130,127	33,368

YEARS. December 31st.	Double or more Lines.	Single Lines.	TOTAL.	TOTAL PAID-UP CAPITAL.	Cost per Mile of Line open.
	Miles.	Miles.	Miles.	£	£
1861	6893	3972	10,865	362,327,338	33,349
1862	7009	4542	11,551	385,218,438	33,349
1863	7270	5052	12,322	404,215,802	32,804
1864	7402	5387	12,789	425,719,613	33,288
1865	7503	5786	13,289	455,478,143	34,275
1866	7711	6143	13,854	481,872,184	34,782
1867	7844	6403	14,247	502,262,887	35,254
1868	7912	6716	14,628	511,680,855	34,979
1869	8124	7021	15,145	518,779,761	34,254
1870	8203	7034	15,237	529,908,673	34,106
1871	8338	7038	15,376	552,661,551	35,943
1872	8512	7302	15,814	569,047,346	35,984
1873	8687	7395	16,082	588,320,308	36,574
1874	8749	7700	16,449	609,895,931	37,078
1875	8898	7760	16,658	630,223,494	37,833
1876	9169	7703	16,872	658,214,776	39,012
1877	9235	7842	17,077	674,059,048	39,472
1878	9412	7921	17,333	698,545,154	40,301

Railways in England, Scotland, and Ireland.

Roughly speaking, about five-eighths of the railways of the United Kingdom, with their invested capital, belong to England and Wales, two - eighths to Scotland, and one - eighth to Ireland. The following tabular statement gives the length of lines, double and single, in each of three divisions of the United Kingdom, the total paid-up capital, cost of construction, and the cost per mile, on the 31st of December, 1878 :—

DIVISIONS.	Double or more Lines.	Single Lines.	TOTAL.	TOTAL PAID-UP CAPITAL.	Cost per Mile of Line open.
	Miles.	Miles.	Miles.	£	£
England and Wales ..	7,758	4,471	12,229	579,387,630	47,378
Scotland ..	1,108	1,737	2,845	87,189,068	30,646
Ireland	546	1,713	2,259	31,968,456	14,151
Total ..	9,412	7,921	17,333	698,545,154	40,301

The few figures here given show that Scotland and Ireland constructed their railways at much less cost than England—Ireland at less than one-third—and also indicate the reason of this diminution of expenditure. In England the railways with double or more lines are nearly twice as numerous as the single lines; while in Scotland the single lines predominate, and in Ireland the single are three times as numerous as the double lines. It is held by all engineers and others conversant with the subject that, whatever other capital may have been misspent, that invested in the construction of double or more lines was a wise outlay. It is in the nature of railways to expand, growing with the growth of population, and it is far cheaper to lay a double track, or more than two lines, at the first construction of a railway, than to add fresh lines afterwards, involving the purchase of land, greatly increased in value through the very fact of the existence of the railway.

It is interesting to consider how the enormous capital invested in the railways of the United Kingdom—not far off the total amount of the National Debt—has been raised. As is well known, the capital of all railway companies is divided into paid-up stock and share capital, represented by what are generally called "shares," subject to fluctuating dividends, and into capital raised by loans and debenture stock,

Railway capital.

the latter bearing a fixed interest, and forming a sort of mortgage upon the revenues. There is a further important subdivision. The paid-up stock and share capital is, in all large companies, divided into "ordinary," "guaranteed," and "preferential" shares, while the capital raised by loans is also distinguished as that of simple "loans" and of "debenture stock." The following two tables exhibit the relative amounts of paid-up share capital and of loan capital raised in each division of the United Kingdom on the 31st of December, 1878 :—

Divisions.	Paid-up Stock and Share Capital.			
	Ordinary.	Guaranteed.	Preferential.	Total Paid-up Stock and Share Capital.
	£	£	£	£
England and Wales ..	218,086,760	75,433,736	139,302,465	432,822,961
Scotland ..	31,257,419	10,273,616	25,958,751	67,489,786
Ireland ..	16,331,161	413,810	7,234,768	23,979,739
Total ..	265,675,340	86,121,162	172,495,984	524,292,486

Divisions.	Capital raised by Loans and Debenture Stock.			Total Capital paid up and raised by Loans and Debenture Stock.
	Loans.	Debenture Stock.	Total raised by Loans and Debenture Stock.	
	£	£	£	£
England and Wales ..	12,591,027	133,973,642	146,564,669	579,387,630
Scotland ..	9,822,066	9,877,216	19,699,282	87,189,068
Ireland ..	1,973,903	6,014,814	7,988,717	31,968,456
Total ..	24,386,996	149,865,672	174,252,668	698,545,154

Dividends of companies.

Very large dividends were paid by some of the earlier railways to their shareholders, but they have become quite exceptional now. At present the average interest on the paid-up capital of the railways of the United Kingdom is barely 4 per cent. Taking together the ordinary, the guaranteed, and the preferential shares, the average interest paid on them in the year 1878 was about $4\frac{1}{4}$ per cent. in England and Wales, while it was only $3\frac{1}{2}$ per cent. in Scotland, and $3\frac{1}{4}$ per cent. in Ireland. As regards the loan capital, including ordinary loan and debenture stock, the average interest paid is somewhat above 4 per cent., but subject likewise, as well as the dividends on the share capital, to fluctuations, with a general tendency in a downward direction. In recent years many of the smaller railway companies have been unable to pay interest on their loan capital, thus reducing the general average, which at one time was 5 per cent. There can be very little doubt that our railways, as at present managed, with their constantly increasing capital funds, and not at all proportionate increase of revenue, must gradually become less and less remunerative. If the growth of capital continue the same for the next ten years as it has been for the preceding decennial period, with no greater increase of traffic and revenue, it is quite certain that at the end of the next ten years the average return upon railway investments, whether share or loan capital, will be barely 3 per cent.

Number of
railway
companies.

There were, according to the last official
"Railway Returns" of the Board of Trade,
issued in 1879, no less than 224 railway companies in the United Kingdom at the end of
1878, exclusive of undertakings the lines of
which were leased to, or worked by, other companies. Of the total, 168 companies were in
England and Wales, 17 in Scotland, and 39 in
Ireland. A process of amalgamation, under
which the smaller lines are gradually absorbed
by the larger railways, has been going on for
many years; still, as will be seen, the total
number of companies is prodigiously large,
especially in England. However insignificant
the company, it has usually its own board of
directors and officials, and the total number of
such "boards" may be put at considerably over
224, as many of the small lines leased or worked
by other companies have still "directors" who,
if not useful, are retained as ornamental, and
mostly draw salaries. But very few of the small
independent lines pay any dividends to their
shareholders, and a large portion of them are
hopelessly bankrupt. This is the reason, no
doubt, why the process of amalgamation has not
been proceeding faster in recent years than it
otherwise might have done. However eager to
extend their own systems, their traffic, and their
revenues, large railway companies are naturally
reluctant to connect themselves with insolvent

concerns, the income of which has little chance, at least under the present mode of railway management, of ever meeting the expenditure. So it has come to pass that, after constant absorption of small lines by the larger railways, some by absolute purchase, some by leases, and many by working agreements—the Great Western Railway, for example, holding at this moment no less than forty-two smaller lines under leases, or working the traffic—there are still 224 railway companies in the United Kingdom.

However, if there be nominally 224 distinct railway undertakings, independent of each other, the bulk of the railways of the United Kingdom belong to twenty chief companies. Of these there are ten in England and Wales, owning 10,015 miles, out of a total of 12,229 miles; five in Scotland, possessed of 2773 miles, out of a total of 2845; and five in Ireland, controlling 1723 miles, out of a total of 2259 miles. The following is a list of these twenty chief companies, in each of the divisions of the United Kingdom, arranged in order of the extent of their mileage, with the addition of the share and loan capital, and the aggregate of both, of each company, as returned for the 31st December, 1878:—

ENGLAND AND WALES.

RAILWAY COMPANIES.	Length of System.	Stock and Share Capital.	Loan Capital.	TOTAL Paid-up Capital.
	Miles.	£	£	£
1. Great Western	2,139	47,745,382	16,434,381	64,179,763
2. London and North-Western	1,676	68,828,782	21,789,326	90,618,108
3. North-Eastern	1,453	41,828,729	12,814,327	54,643,076
4. Midland	1,295	49,790,810	14,836,887	64,627,697
5. Great Eastern	877	21,218,236	10,646,726	31,864,962
6. London and South-Western	698	16,545,007	6,180,910	22,725,917
7. Great Northern ..	693	23,058,432	7,323,845	30,382,277
8. Lancashire and Yorkshire	455	23,466,958	7,531,173	30,998,131
9. London, Brighton, and South Coast	349	15,158,584	5,023,982	20,182,566
10. South-Eastern	334	14,834,088	4,919,790	19,753,878

SCOTLAND.

RAILWAY COMPANIES.	Length of System.	Stock and Share Capital.	Loan Capital.	TOTAL Paid-up Capital.
	Miles.	£	£	£
1. North British	913	21,518,020	7,208,414	28,726,434
2. Caledonian	847	26,145,014	6,920,674	33,065,688
3. Highland	402	2,635,577	800,480	3,436,057
4. Glasgow and South-Western	325	7,230,050	2,230,938	9,460,988
5. Great North of Scotland	286	2,600,552	956,877	3,557,429

IRELAND.

RAILWAY COMPANIES.	Length of System.	Stock and Share Capital.	Loan Capital.	TOTAL Paid-up Capital.
	Miles.	£	£	£
1. Great Southern and Western	486	6,181,652	933,965	7,115,617
2. Great Northern of Ireland	450	4,001,270	1,302,363	5,303,633
3. Midland Great Western	425	3,057,014	1,350,907	4,407,921
4. Waterford and Limerick	202	1,398,325	561,508	1,959,833
5. Belfast and Northern Counties	151	1,198,900	417,381	1,616,281

Large and small companies.

To the question, "Should our railways be private or national property?" a first practical answer is given by an examination of the comparative dividends of large and small railway companies. It has been already stated that the mass of the 224 railway companies of the United Kingdom pay no dividend at all, and that a great number of them are hopelessly insolvent. As a rule, it may be said that the smaller the company the less profitable the undertaking. The same holds good, with very few exceptions, as regards the great companies, the rule being that the larger the company the higher the dividends, and, what is not unimportant, the *safer* the dividends. This will be found to be the case on examining the financial position of the leading railway companies of England, Scotland, and Ireland, enumerated in the preceding tables.

At the head of English companies, as far as mileage gives the rank, stands the Great Western. But it is not really the largest company, its capital being very much less than that of the London and North-Western, while the 2139 miles of the system are to the extent of just one-half single lines. The Great Western in fact has risen to the place it holds by the amalgamation of a mass of small lines with the original system,—and has thus risen to the manifest advantage of its shareholders. The growth is that of the last twenty years, when the process of amalgamation commenced on a considerable scale. In the latter part of 1858, the company was at its lowest depth, the directors declaring, in September of that year, that they were not

The Great Western Railway.

able to pay any dividend at all on the ordinary shares; but from that period, with the growth of the undertaking, the company gradually righted itself, paying successively annual dividends of 2, 3, 4, and 5 per cent. The very extent of the network of lines controlled by the Great Western is now generally looked upon by investors as a guarantee of the dividend-paying power of the company.

The London and North-Western.

Nominally next in extent of mileage to the Great Western, but really the first of English railway companies, stands the London and North - Western. Its 1676 miles of railway consist to the extent of nearly three-fourths of double or more lines, there being no more than 382 miles of single lines. The huge share and loan capital of the London and North-Western, 90,618,108*l.*, does not even quite represent the total amount of money raised by this great company, for, in addition, figure subscriptions of 3,538,642*l.* made to smaller companies, destined ultimately to join the vast network of lines embraced by the system. As it is the largest, so the London and North-Western is likewise the most prosperous of railway companies. Investment in the shares of the company is regarded generally to be nearly as safe as investment in the Funds; it has loans outstanding at $3\frac{1}{2}$ and $3\frac{3}{4}$ per cent., and quite recently was able to effect the conversion of all its guaranteed and preference shares, some bearing rather high rates, into uniform 4 per cent. Stocks. The London and North-Western Company, offspring of the genius of the "father of railways," George Stephenson —whose marble statue worthily fills the centre of the magnificent hall of Euston Station— furnishes in its own history the most striking proof of the advantages of a large system of lines well organized and well managed. The argument that all the railways of the kingdom should be under unity of administration is irresistible, considering these facts. Of course, the union can never be brought about by private energy, struggling against a thousandfold conflicting interests, but it must be achieved, as a national concern, by the Government of the country.

The third of English railway companies, the North-Eastern, offers in its way almost as interesting an example as the London and North-Western of the advantages of a large system judiciously managed. The North-Eastern, with its 1453 miles of railway, 948 consisting of double, or more, and 505 of single lines, is the upshot of a series of amalgamations, the original undertaking, called the "Great North of England," having attracted to itself a number of smaller railways. Since these amalgamations took place, but not before, the North-Eastern has been highly prosperous. From 1856 to 1869, the annual dividends of the company gradually rose from 4 per cent. to 6 per cent.; they reached $7\frac{1}{4}$ per cent. in 1870, $8\frac{1}{2}$ per cent.

The North-Eastern Railway.

in 1871, and 10 per cent. in 1872. Since then, there has been a slight falling off in the dividend-paying power of the company, caused by the depression of trade, felt chiefly in the manufacturing districts embraced by the system; but the decline is clearly only temporary. Like the shares of the London and North-Western, those of the North-Eastern Company are considered "as good as Consols." The company has loans outstanding at $3\frac{3}{4}$ per cent. interest, and the bulk of its guaranteed shares has been raised at 4 per cent. interest. It may be mentioned here that nearly all the small companies within the same district served by the North-Eastern succumbed under the depression of trade felt in recent years, a sufficient exemplification of the value of the proverb, that "union is strength," as applied to railways.

The Midland Railway.

But perhaps the fourth of English railways, the Midland, furnishes a more striking proof than even the North-Eastern of the immense advantages of union and combination. The Midland, now a gigantic system embracing 1295 miles, of which 926 consist of double or more lines, and only 369 of single lines, was in its origin a purely local undertaking. When George Stephenson was planning railways in the midland counties, he met one day Mr. John Ellis, a farmer near Leicester, and a member of the Society of Friends. Desirous of purchasing some of his land, George Stephenson explained to Mr. Ellis the prospects of railways, present and future; and the shrewd Quaker farmer was so much struck by what he was told that he not only invested the whole of his own fortune in railway shares, but induced a great number of his own body, wealthy men most of them, to do the same. Under the careful management of Mr. John Ellis, first chairman of the nucleus of lines which grew up near Leicester, the "Midland" soon attracted other less prosperous lines within its fold, till after the lapse of little over a quarter of a century it has now developed into a vast system, the main lines of which connect London with Scotland, throwing out branches in all directions, far into the West of England, and developing more than any other railway the mineral wealth of England by an enormous coal traffic. But a few years ago, the Midland was compelled to run its trains southwards over the Great Northern Railway. Now the company has its own palatial Metropolitan terminus at St. Pancras, in the shadow of which the Great Northern looks small. It is a curious fact that the first English railway, from Stockton to Darlington, opened in 1825, was constructed mainly by the aid of money furnished by Quakers; so was also the origin of the third and the fourth greatest of English railways due to the foresight and energy of members of the Society of Friends. The North-Eastern and the Midland both grew up under the direction of

Quakers. The son of Mr. John Ellis, Mr. Edward Shipley Ellis, succeeded his father as chairman of the Midland Company, and still rules its destinies. Perhaps if a member of the Society of Friends were to be called into the Cabinet, he might be the means of securing the union of the whole of the railways of the kingdom under unity of administration.

The Great Eastern Railway.

Not directly illustrative of the advantage of large systems of lines, but nevertheless indirectly showing quite the same result on the other side, is the position of the fifth of English railways, the Great Eastern. The Great Eastern Company, possessing 877 miles of railway, of which about one-half are single lines, has for the last fifteen years either paid no dividends at all to the holders of its ordinary shares, or very trifling ones. The cause of this want of success is perfectly clear, and admitted on all hands. Its lines running through the eastern counties of England, for the most part purely agricultural and filled with a comparatively sparse population, the Great Eastern Railway, although constructed cheaply, running over level ground, cannot exist by itself. To prosper, it must be united with the railway systems of central England, more particularly the North-Eastern and Great Northern, so as to be able to carry the agricultural produce of its own districts at low rates to the busy hives of the northern and midland counties, and to let the trains, carrying it, bring back coal and manufactured goods. The whole question is so simple that one wonders it has not been brought long ago to a favourable result. That this has not been the case is owing simply to inveterate jealousy of railway companies of each other. Unceasing efforts have been made for the last five years to bring about an amalgamation of the Great Eastern with the North-Eastern and Great Northern—the latter two virtually under one supreme direction—but hitherto without any result. It is doubtful whether the union, undoubtedly profitable to all parties concerned, will be effected before the time, which must arrive, when Government takes the matter in hand, having become persuaded that private advantages must give way to the public interest.

Of the sixth of English railways, the London and South-Western, but little need be said. It is fairly prosperous, but might be far more so if united either with the other lines starting from the Metropolis south of the river Thames, or with the Great Western. The London and South-Western Company, possessed of 698 miles of line, of which 478 are double and 220 single, has a very profitable suburban traffic, but the profits thus made are squandered, to a great extent, in needless competition with the Great Western for the West of England traffic, necessitating tremendous speed of trains, many of which must run at a loss. Other great companies, it is true, play the same losing game,—

of this more will have to be said anon—but the London and South-Western, a comparatively small undertaking, can less afford to do so than its giant brethren. As it is, though not under the repute of excellent management, it pays its 5 and 6 per cent. dividends with much regularity, and can borrow money on loans at from $3\frac{1}{2}$ to $4\frac{1}{2}$ per cent. But to obtain these results, the company has to charge very high rates, both for goods and passengers, which could be abandoned by amalgamation with other railways, resulting in greatly decreased expenditure.

The Great Northern Railway.

The seventh of English railway companies, the Great Northern, has its fortunes cast in to a great extent, as already noticed, with the North-Eastern. The two companies wisely work together, and enjoy the advantages derived therefrom. By itself, the Great Northern is an amalgamation of about a dozen railways, the number including the "East Lincolnshire," the "Holme and Ramsay," the "South and East Coast," and other lines. Regular dividends of from 4 to 7 per cent. paid to the holders of ordinary shares, and loans raised at 4 per cent., show the advantages which the Great Northern has derived from its union with the North-Eastern Company. It is but one more illustration of the profits of union.

The Lancashire and Yorkshire.

Like the Great Northern, the eighth in rank of English railway companies, the Lancashire and Yorkshire, which has its headquarters at Manchester, is fairly prosperous, through the wisdom of its managers of working together with other lines. Actual amalgamation would undoubtedly be better, and more. profitable to the shareholders, the line serving some of the busiest and most populous districts of the kingdom. The amount of traffic on the Lancashire and Yorkshire is indicated by the fact that it has fewer single lines than any other railway, not only in England, but in the world. The total length of the system comprises 455 miles, and of these 437 miles consist of double or more lines, and only 18 miles, representing short branches, of single lines. The Lancashire and Yorkshire Railway has always paid good dividends, varying in recent years from $5\frac{1}{2}$ per cent. to 8 per cent. With amalgamation, which would greatly reduce the expenditure, the net profits of such a line as this would certainly be at least 10 per cent. It involves an absolutely needless waste of money to constitute a large body of directors—the " board " of the Lancashire and Yorkshire is composed of no less than sixteen of these exalted personages—with full administrative staff for a railway, the total length of which is under 500 miles.

What is true in this respect for the Manchester Company is still more so for the two railways south of the Thames, the headquarters of which are at London Bridge. The London, *The London, Brighton, and South Coast.*

Brighton, and South Coast, and the South-Eastern, ninth and tenth in the list of English railway companies, the first with 349 miles of line, and the other with 334 miles, are undertakings which, if reason guided the shareholders instead of prejudice, and, in most instances, senseless apathy, ought to have united long ago. The lines of the two companies serve the same district, the agricultural counties of Kent and Sussex, and at many points, such as Hastings, Tunbridge Wells, and others, the trains, each usually not one-half filled, run side by side. As there are two sets of trains, where one might do, so there are two boards of directors, highly salaried, especially in the case of the South-Eastern, and two complete administrative staffs, with secretaries, managers, engineers, architects, and so forth. Who pays for all this? Simply the public.

High fares.

For the most part the fares on all the lines served by these two last-mentioned companies are enormously high; for if they compete otherwise, they are in happy agreement as to the policy of charging the highest sums they possibly can to the ordinary travellers, season-ticket holders, and others who are compelled to make use of their trains. Of course, the shareholders are contented as long as they get good dividends, and but few of them strive to consider that the system pursued is a matter of public far more than of private interest. The London, Brighton, and South

Coast, and South-Eastern proprietors, drawing 6 and 7 per cent. dividends, are naturally happy men, and inclined for nothing else than to sing "*laissez faire, laissez aller.*" If this be human on their part, it is still surprising that the shareholders of another company running alongside the South - Eastern, the unfortunate London, Chatham, and Dover line, should not insist upon amalgamation. The London, Chatham, and Dover Railway has never once since it was opened for traffic returned a dividend to its shareholders, and probably never will as long as it is merely private property, managed as at present. Notwithstanding its impecuniosity, the company runs twice a day express trains from London to Dover and back, precisely at the same hours as the South-Eastern, the rival trains—each generally not half filled—speeding along at the rate of fifty miles an hour, and at proportionate cost. That this should be allowed to go on can be explained only, if at all, by the fact of the unlucky sharehoders of the ill-starred London, Chatham, and Dover line having lost all hope of ever getting a return for their investments, and that they have thus become quite indifferent to its fate. Thus one set of shareholders is unconcerned through prosperity, and another through adversity. By all, the public interest is left entirely out of consideration.

Having gone through a review of the condition of the principal railway companies of England, Scottish railways.

those of Scotland and Ireland may pass under examination. It need be but a short one. England's railways embrace a total of 12,229 miles, while Scotland has only 2845 miles of lines, and Ireland but 2259 miles. Besides this, the companies of the other two divisions of the United Kingdom are small compared with those of England. The leading Scottish railway company, the North British, with its headquarters at Edinburgh, rules 913 miles, but of these 522 miles are single lines, and only 391 double. For many years the North British returned no dividends to its ordinary shareholders, and more recently those paid have been but trifling. Financially better is the position of the Caledonian, second of Scottish railway companies, with headquarters at Glasgow, which has 847 miles, of which 452 miles are double and 395 single lines. The Caledonian last year paid a $4\frac{1}{2}$ per cent. dividend to some of its shareholders, but not to all. Holders of so-called " deferred ordinary stock "— a title given to one of the many new manipulations to which railway property has been subjected in recent years—received no dividends, and on the whole the condition of the Caledonian is far from satisfactory. The really most prosperous of Scottish railway companies is the one ranking third as regards mileage, the Highland, which has Inverness for headquarters. It is prosperous because built at a small cost, all the lines being single, with the exception of seven miles, representing stations and sidings. Taking paid-up capital and mileage, the Caledonian Railway had its property constructed at 39,000*l*. per mile, while that of the Highland Company stands at only 8500*l*. per mile. The result is shown in pretty regular dividends of about 5 per cent. per annum. The fourth of Scottish railways, the Glasgow and South-Western, running from Glasgow to Carlisle, with a few branches, is also a fairly prosperous line, but chiefly so through being worked in connection with the Midland Railway Company, which runs its trains over it to the north. Without this alliance, the shareholders would scarcely get the dividends, ranging from $3\frac{1}{2}$ to 4 per cent., which they received in recent years. There are no dividends for the fifth of Scottish lines, the Great North of Scotland Railway Company, which has its seat at Aberdeen. Like the Highland, the Great North of Scotland Railway was built at comparatively small cost, consisting of only single lines, with the exception of stations, but still it will not thrive, simply for want of intimate union with other lines. It is strange to think that so shrewd a people as Scotchmen are presumed to be should not long ago have brought about an amalgamation of the whole of their railways. All the lines of North Britain together, making allowance for the fact of many of them being only single, do not come up to the real mileage of the Great Western of Eng-

Midland Great Western of Ireland, also with headquarters at Dublin, owning 425 miles, 294 of them single and 131 miles double lines, usually pays dividends between $4\frac{1}{2}$ and 5 per cent.; but the company next in the list, the Waterford and Limerick, does not return quite 3 per cent. to its shareholders, although its paid-up capital is very small, representing not more than 9700*l.* per mile of railway, the track consisting almost entirely of single lines. Most prosperous of Irish railway companies is the fifth in rank, the Belfast and Northern Counties, but its success is due to exceptional circumstances. Scottish energy and the flourishing linen trade of the north of Ireland have made the prosperity of a little railway, cheaply constructed, and mainly a single line, so that its shareholders have been enabled to draw, in recent years, dividends ranging from $6\frac{1}{2}$ to $7\frac{1}{2}$ per cent. But the usual railway waste has prevailed here also, as everywhere else, together with a good revenue. Though but 151 miles long, the Belfast and Northern Counties Railway needs, to be kept working, a board of twelve directors, a general manager, a secretary, and a large staff of administrative officers. It seems a farce, and would be ludicrous if the effects of the farce, repeated all over the United Kingdom, were not of such serious import to the nation.

In the preceding sketch of English, Scottish, and Irish railways, only twenty of the leading   Minor railway companies.

companies, it will be seen, have been referred to as worthy of notice, out of the total of 224 companies enumerated in the last annual " Railway Returns " issued by the Board of Trade. Some idea of the nature and position of the majority of the two hundred and more small railways which exist in the United Kingdom may be formed from the following tabular statement, giving, in alphabetical order, the names of a number of English companies, and length of their lines, together with the number of their directors, their authorized and paid-up capital, and the interest and dividends paid on such capital, distinguishing that raised by loans from that raised by shares, in the year 1878 :—

Specimens of small English railway companies.

RAILWAY COMPANIES.	Length of Line.	Number of Directors.	Authorized Capital.	Total Paid-up Capital	Interest on Loan Capital.	Dividends on Share Capital.
	miles.		£	£	per ct.	per ct.
Abbotsbury	6	4	72,000	5,594	nil.	nil.
Aylesbury and Bucking-ham	12	9	291,500	119,089	5	nil.
Bala and Festiniog	18	8	253,300	48,170	nil.	nil.
Barnoldswick	2	5	53,300	30,845	4	nil.
Birmingham and Lichfield	8	5	180,000	1,500	nil.	nil.
Bishop's Castle	19	4	629,000	309,709	5	nil.
Bodmin and Wadebridge	15	10	35,500	35,500	nil.	nil.
Brewood and Wolverhamp-ton	2	5	33,000	1,400	nil.	nil.
Bristol Port	6	4	166,000	166,000	5	nil.
Bury and Tottington ..	4	5	76,000	16,105	nil.	nil.
Carmarthen and Cardigan	19	9	902,200	756,683	5	nil.
Charnwood Forest	11	7	212,000	8,641	nil.	nil.
Clacton-on-Sea	4	3	33,300	8,275	nil.	nil.
Cleator and Workington	15	8	284,000	186,296	4	nil.
Cleveland Extension ..	11	4	226,000	19,697	6	nil.
Coleford	5	3	88,000	21,700	nil.	nil.
Colne Valley and Halstead	19	6	289,600	204,474	5	nil.
Cowes and Newport ..	5	4	119,800	80,365	5	nil.
Cranbrook and Paddock Wood	13	7	133,000	2,980	nil.	nil.

Railway Companies.	Length of Line.	Number of Directors.	Authorized Capital.	Total Paid-up Capital.	Interest on Loan Capital.	Dividends on Share Capital.
	miles.		£	£	per ct.	per ct.
Devon and Cornwall ..	13	10	746,000	178,680	nil.	nil.
East Cornwall	7	4	346,660	80,000	5	nil.
East Norfolk	14	9	306,600	275,640	4½	nil.
Ely and Bury St. Edmunds	23	6	133,300	4,766	nil.	nil.
Felixstowe	13	8	226,600	130,000	nil.	nil.
Festiniog and Blaenan ..	4	6	32,550	24,032	4¾	nil.
Garstang and Knot End ..	11	4	120,000	96,605	5	nil.
Great Marlow	3	5	24,000	23,000	5	nil.
Halesowen	7	4	220,000	159,296	5	nil.
Hunstanton and West Norfolk	15	6	260,000	200,000	4½	2
Isle of Wight	12	6	226,600	155,925	5	nil.
Liskeard and Carados ..	8	8	40,825	40,825	4½	3
Lostwithiel and Towey ..	5	6	40,000	34,536	6	nil.
Louth and Lincoln	22	5	401,000	396,250	5	nil.
Ludlow and Clee Hill ..	6	6	42,000	42,000	5	nil.
Lynn and Fakenham ..	21	5	200,000	51,889	nil.	nil.
Manchester and Milford ..	42	6	800,400	715,455	5	nil.
Market Deeping	3	4	20,000	235	nil.	nil.
Milford Haven	2	6	186,000	119,711	5	nil.
North Wales	10	7	141,300	103,515	5	nil.
Pembroke and Tenby ..	29	7	552,200	446,988	4½	nil.
Ravenglass and Eskdale	7	6	48,000	32,000	6	nil.
Ross and Ledbury	12	4	240,000	36,000	nil.	nil.
Ryde and Newport	8	5	206,600	171,740	5	nil.
Scarborough and Whitby	20	5	226,000	36,087	nil.	nil.
Severn Bridge	5	8	433,300	332,098	4½	nil.
Snaibeach District	5	6	26,600	21,320	4½	3
South Wales	12	9	250,210	205,960	5	nil.
Stafford and Uttoxeter ..	13	6	239,900	293,385	5	nil.
Swindon and Andover ..	26	10	500,000	14,746	nil.	nil.
Tees Valley	7	9	82,600	81,011	4½	2
Thetford and Watton ..	9	5	105,300	85,866	5	nil.
Tottenham and Hampstead	6	9	510,000	417,000	4½	nil.
Vale of Towy	11	6	78,000	73,000	4½	5
West Lancashire	14	7	649,960	101,745	nil.	nil.
West Somerset Mineral ..	12	5	105,000	105,000	5	5
Wigan Junction	11	5	600,000	140,080	nil.	nil.
Yarmouth and Norfolk ..	17	4	210,600	93,082	5	4

The railways here enumerated, 57 in number, all in England and Wales, are specimens, selected at random, of the two hundred and more small companies existing in the United Kingdom, the great majority of which are possessed of no vitality, that is, no dividend-paying power, chiefly because the cost of their management is out of all proportion to their possible earnings. It will be seen that there are railway companies the lines of which are but two, three, and four miles in length, which have "boards" of five and even six directors. It may be that often "in the multitude of counsellors there is safety," but the saying can scarcely be applied to our railway counsellors and administrators.

Number of railway directors

There are at this moment over one thousand directors administering the railways of the United Kingdom, the mass of them presiding over the affairs of some single small line, but a certain number uniting in their own persons the directorship of a dozen and more lines, great and small. No fewer than forty-four members of the House of Lords and one hundred and eighteen members of the House of Commons are railway directors. It cannot be denied, therefore, that the "railway interest" is well represented in our legislature, and the only question is whether such "interest," which is after all but that of private trading companies endeavouring to earn as much money as possible, is always cognate with, and not sometimes adverse to, the public and national welfare.

High rates and fares.

The multiplicity of railways, number of directors, and diversity of management have led to the almost inevitable consequence of varying charges for goods and passengers, and of strangely differing proportions of revenue and expenditure. To what an extent even the leading railway companies of the United Kingdom differ as regards their receipts and expenses, may be seen from the subjoined two series of tables, published on the authority of the Board of Trade in the last official " General Report on the Railway Companies," issued in August 1879. The first series of tables exhibits a comparison of the receipts per train-mile, and the second the proportion of expenditure to receipts of the ten leading English railways before specified, and of one great Scottish and one Irish line in the years 1858 and 1870, as well as in the seven years from 1872 to 1878 :—

RECEIPTS PER TRAIN-MILE.

Receipts of twelve leading companies.

Years.	Great Western.	London and North-Western.	North-Eastern.	Midland.	Great Eastern.	London and South-Western.
	d.	d.	d.	d.	d.	d.
1858	69·16	77·43	52·71	61·67	67·43	65·45
1870	63·43	66·31	65·55	52·31	63·55	63·84
1872	64·11	66·67	67·31	63·55	65·89	65·46
1873	66·36	68·66	71·63	69·41	67·43	67·47
1874	66·85	69·58	71·78	65·99	68·97	67·69
1875	65·90	68·83	71·47	63·27	66·29	66·85
1876	64·69	67·77	70·36	62·71	66·62	65·37
1877	64·43	67·62	69·77	60·89	64·18	67·92
1878	62·89	67·86	69·64	59·55	65·30	65·94

Years.	Great Northern.	Lancashire and Yorkshire,	London, Brighton, and South Coast.	South-Eastern.	Caledonian.	Great Southern and Western of Ireland.
	d.	d.	d.	d.	d.	d.
1858	56·29	73·24	85·53	88·87	61·74	73·55
1870	57·28	64·23	66·69	84·20	49·74	62·49
1872	59·71	69·36	66·83	90·28	55·55	68·00
1873	64·05	72·79	70·26	91·61	58·99	67·41
1874	64·38	71·53	70·57	91·96	62·56	66·94
1875	62·52	74·44	69·97	91·47	63·02	69·58
1876	60·82	74·83	67·77	87·91	61·88	71·66
1877	60·10	75·33	67·36	88·59	60·46	69·62
1878	58·44	75·00	66·87	85·73	58·20	68·66

PROPORTION OF EXPENDITURE TO RECEIPTS.

Years.	Great Western.	London and North-Western.	North-Eastern.	Midland.	Great Eastern.	London and South-Western.
	Per cent.	Per cent.	Per cent.	Per cent.	Per cent.	Per cent.
1858	42	54	42	42	50	46
1870	47	47	46	47	50	54
1872	46	47	54	47	52	55
1873	49	52	53	52	57	58
1874	51	55	56	55	57	60
1875	51	55	54	54	58	55
1876	52	54	55	54	54	56
1877	52	54	55	54	57	55
1878	51	53	53	53	55	55

Years.	Great Northern.	Lancashire and Yorkshire.	London, Brighton, and South Coast.	South-Eastern.	Caledonian.	Great Southern and Western of Ireland.
	Per cent.	Per cent.	Per cent.	Per cent.	Per cent.	Per cent.
1858	52	43	46	49	43	39
1870	49	48	52	47	50	51
1872	51	49	50	47	52	50
1873	55	56	52	49	55	56
1874	55	59	51	51	56	57
1875	55	58	49	49	51	55
1876	56	57	49	48	51	53
1877	57	54	49	47	52	54
1878	56	54	49	48	51	54

The figures in the preceding tables require studying, and when this is done they will be found to be highly instructive as regards the management of our principal lines of railways. First of all, it will be seen that the general earnings of nearly all the principal companies, expressed per train-mile, have decreased largely in the twenty years from 1858 to 1878. For example, the Great Western Railway, which had a revenue of 5*s.* 9*d.* per train-mile in 1858, only took 5*s.* 2*d.* in 1878, while the decrease in the case of the London and North-Western, virtually the leader of all the railway companies of the

United Kingdom, was from 6*s*. 5*d*. in 1858 to 5*s*. 7*d*. in 1878. The takings per train-mile, it will be noticed, were always larger, and continue so to this time, on the South-Eastern than on any other line of railway. They were 7*s*. 4*d*. per train-mile in 1858, and continued at 7*s*. 1*d*. in 1878. High, and in many instances exorbitant fares furnish the explanation. In respect to the proportion of expenditure to receipts, a very momentous factor in railway management, it is curious to notice the striking differences that exist between many of the railways. While one company disburses but 48 per cent. of its revenue in working expenses, another requires 56 per cent. It will be seen also that, with the exception of but two companies in the list, the proportion of expenditure to receipts greatly rose in the twenty years from 1858 to 1878. It is admitted by all who are conversant with railway management that the average proportion of expenditure to receipts is far too high on all the railways. It ought to be nearer 30 per cent. than 50, and could be reduced doubtlessly to the former figure if the two hundred and odd companies, with their thousand directors, were to be brought under one general management.

Want of unity in management and opposing influences on the part of the great as well as the small companies, leading each to seek their own interests only, without the slightest regard to that of their clients the public, have hitherto been the main cause why the railways of this country have been very far from being of such universal advantage to the nation as they might be, if well organized. The charges are far too high both for passengers and goods, and as a consequence the whole traffic is very inefficiently developed.

According to the " Railway Returns " of the Board of Trade, the total number of travellers, first, second, and third class, carried by the railways of the United Kingdom, was as follows in the year 1878 :—

—	1st Class.	2nd Class.	3rd Class.	TOTAL.
England and Wales ..	34,737,267	57,562,107	411,683,519	503,982,893
Scotland ..	4,815,298	3,578,233	34,766,885	43,160,416
Ireland ..	1,833,841	4,204,400	11,842,905	17,881,146
Total United Kingdom	41,386,406	65,344,740	458,293,309	565,024,455

Looked at superficially, the number of 565,000,000 passengers carried in one year by the railways of the United Kingdom may seem large, but it is really not so if the figures be properly analyzed. The population of the kingdom in the middle of 1878 was estimated at 33,882,000, and therefore the total railway traffic was somewhat less than seventeen times the population. Now the traffic on many lines, traversing, it may be, thickly populated parts of the country, but not having by any means a " monopoly of communication," is double, treble, and fourfold the amount. The short railway, only 24 miles in length, owned by the company known as the Sheffield and Midland Committee, carried by itself $2\frac{3}{4}$ millions of passengers, nearly the whole third class, in the year 1878, and there are numerous similar instances to show that, provided the fares be sufficiently low, the influx of travellers is practically unlimited. The Metropolitan Railway carried $52\frac{1}{2}$ millions of passengers in the year 1878; the Metropolitan District $29\frac{1}{2}$ millions; and the North London 27 millions in the same year. Thus the railways of the Metropolis north of the Thames alone, 34 miles in length altogether, carried 109 millions of people in one year. One has only to look at the crowded trains called "excursions," swarming with human beings, not a seat being unoccupied, to see the carrying capacity—and, truly also, the money-earning capacity—of our railways. But the thousand gentlemen, noble lords included, who now direct the management of the iron highroads of this country, do not appear to be able to perceive this simple fact. Instead of running well-filled cheap trains at a moderate rate of speed, their companies vie in organizing terribly expensive fast trains, at exorbitant fares, the carriages of which are mostly empty. One often feels inclined to think that there is a disposition on the part of the directors to assume that railways were brought into existence only for the class to which they themselves belong, the "upper ten." It is superb, no doubt, to fly through space at the rate of fifty miles an hour, in a train of sumptuous first-class carriages. But does it pay? It is like the Balaclava Charge. "*C'est beau, mais ce n'est pas la guerre.*"

Express trains.

All practically conversant with railway management decisively assert that "expresses" do not pay. More and more the fact is becoming undisputed that the most profitable class of railway customers is that going third class, representing the opposite end of the "upper ten." Mr. James Allport, general manager of the Midland —perhaps the most able railway administrator whom this country has yet produced—fully acknowledged this when deciding a few years ago, by a great stroke of dictatorship, to do two things that had never been done before, namely, to add third-class carriages to all the express trains of his line, and to do away with second-class carriages altogether. The success of his innovation was so great that most of the other leading lines had to follow his example after a while. But they did so most reluctantly.

Rates for merchandise.

If the movement of passengers on our lines of railways be restricted by inordinately high fares, the same is the case to an equal degree as regards the movement of goods and merchandise of all kinds. The aggregate amount of goods carried on all the railways of the United Kingdom in the year 1878 was not more than

206,735,856 tons, and of this total very nearly three-fourths consisted of minerals, mainly coals. The weight of goods described as " general merchandise " carried by all the railways of the United Kingdom in 1878 amounted to but 57,774,846 tons, of which 47,331,700 fell to the share of England, 6,685,442 tons to that of Scotland, and 2,757,704 tons to that of Ireland. This gives an annual carriage of only 3870 tons of merchandise per mile in England, of 2310 tons per mile for Scotland, and of 1220 tons per mile in Ireland. It would be waste of time to dwell upon the obvious fact that this work of merchandise-carriers which our railways are now doing is infinitely below what they might do, if properly organized on the basis of an even and greatly reduced tariff. With it, there can be no reasonable doubt that the carriage of goods by railway, more particularly that of small parcels and quantities, would increase as much as the carriage of letters did after the introduction of the uniform penny postage stamp.

In a leader of the 'Times' of August 25th last, in which the report of the London and North-Western Company for the first half-year of 1879 is commented upon, it is justly remarked that on all our railways, " locomotion and the carriage of goods are probably more heavily taxed than in any other country, and our freights form a very appreciable element in the disadvantages under which our agriculture suffers in its competition with America. In provincial towns too, which are supplied with meat, fish, and other necessaries from London, the railway charges add considerably to the cost of living, and local tradesmen are often unfairly blamed for prices which it is beyond their power to modify." The 'Times' hopes that railway companies "may be induced, by depressed trade and low dividends," to "give increased facilities to their clients the public;" but such expectation, as shown by long experience, is perfectly groundless. The directing boards of railway companies are not only selfish in their very essence, but, what is worse, only aim at immediate gain, as regardless of the future as of "their clients the public." To pay the largest possible dividend for the current half-year, or the year, and thereby to keep the shares of the undertaking at high prices, is the main object of every railway board in the kingdom, and to it all else is sacrificed. The means to accomplish this often would not bear scrutiny, but only the initiated few know that there is many a company which for years has paid dividends out of capital instead of *bonâ fide* earnings. What is undeniable is that there exists scarcely a railway company in the country which can be said to have closed its capital account.

Increase of railway capital.

Year after year, on almost all the lines, fresh capital is added to pay for expenses which ought to have come out of the revenue. In order to pay the dividends for which, and for nothing else, the shareholders cry, fresh burthens have constantly to be imposed on the public in the shape of increased rates and fares. Perhaps, at bottom, neither directors nor shareholders are much to blame in the matter. The fault is one inherent to a system under which an agency greatly influencing the well-being, and even the existence of the nation, is left in private hands, a mere matter of commercial speculation, instead of being under the control of the Government of the country. What would be said to the proposal of private companies offering to embank the rivers Thames, Mersey, and Humber, and to levy heavy tolls, at their own discretion, on all the shipping passing up and down these water-highways? The mere idea of it would be pronounced by most men as preposterous. Yet the new land-highways, at least as important as the old water-highways, are thus monopolized for purely private interests. The time will come, and perhaps is not far off, when men will wonder that a people as practical as the British nation should have left for half a century the monopoly of the greatest of modern inventions, that of steam-propelled trains, in private hands for private profit. The irrationality, to future eyes, will be the more glaring, as we acted on a different principle as regards the carrying of messages to that of human beings, and the bulk of the nation's commerce. Letters and telegraphic messages, as if they were sacred things above all others, are carried by the nation for the nation, while the carrying of people themselves and all that they grow, make, and manufacture, is left to commercial undertakers and speculators. All thinking men must agree that this anomaly will have to come to an end, sooner or later. It can be merely a question of time.

Purchase of railways by the State.

The purchase of our railways by the State, beyond doubt, can be merely a question of time. All over Europe the railways are fast becoming national property, and the fate of our own iron highways, deeply important as they are to an essentially trading people, must be the same. It seems quite impossible, and opposed to common sense, that undertakings upon the good management of which, to a considerable extent, the prosperity of the nation depends, should be left subject, as a mere matter of gains or losses, to a certain number of individuals, instead of being handed over to the control of the representatives of the people. However, we are not fond, as a nation, of grappling with high questions of policy at a moment's notice. We left our Indian empire for over two hundred years in the hands of a knot of merchants congregating in Leadenhall Street, and it is no wonder, therefore, that we have left our own iron highroads for half a century at the control of another knot of commercial men, who, quite justly from their own standpoint, keep mainly individual interests in view.

If it be granted that, as with our Indian empire, so with our railways, they cannot fail to become national property, the question arises whether this inevitable event should not be accelerated, rather than delayed, by stimulating public opinion on the subject, and making the nation acquainted with all the facts bearing on the subject. To this end the chief advantages that may accrue from the immediate purchase of railways by the State may be summed up under a few headings.

Advantages of State Railways for the United Kingdom.

1. The possibility of a general lowering of charges both for goods and passengers. There seems no insuperable difficulty that railways, if national property, should not be organized after the model of the Post Office, with a uniform charge, if not for travellers all at once, at least for general merchandise, especially for small parcels, or boxes, say under fifty pounds in weight.

The cost of carrying such parcels is really trifling, and the undoubtedly vast increase of traffic thus created would compensate, and more than compensate, for the withdrawal of the present enormously high, and in many instances prohibitory charges. As regards passengers it might, perhaps, be difficult to establish at once uniform charges, like those now existing for letters and telegrams; still an approach towards such uniformity might be made by a preliminary establishment of *zones* within which the fares would be the same. Ten such zones might suffice for the whole of the United Kingdom, the fares upon which, first and second class, might be somewhat of the following amount. Only two classes are necessary to be taken into account, as it is all but certain that the example of the sagacious general manager of the Midland Railway, who cut off one class from the old-fashioned and quite needless three, must ultimately be adopted. It is needless to say that these proposed zones, with their fares, are merely offered as hints.

Plan of
railway fares
in zones.

Zones.				First Class.				Second Class.	
				s.	*d.*			*s.*	*d.*
Under	5 miles	..	..	0	3	..	..	0	2
„	10 „	..	..	0	5	..	..	0	3
„	25 „	..	..	0	8	..	..	0	5
„	50 „	..	..	1	0	..	..	0	8
„	100 „	..	..	1	6	..	..	1	0
„	200 „	..	..	2	0	..	..	1	6
„	300 „	..	..	3	0	..	..	2	0
„	400 „	..	..	4	0	..	..	3	0
„	500 „	..	..	5	0	..	..	4	0
Above	500 „	..	..	6	0	..	..	5	0

Low fares
would be
as productive
as penny
postage.

The impetus given to railway travelling, were there some system tending towards uniformity as that here sketched out, would certainly be enormous, commensurate at least with the increase of the work of the Post Office after the adoption of the penny postage. Millions who now do not travel for want of means, would then come to fill the trains. That it would pay to carry these millions is quite certain. Our railway companies now carry a ton of coals, with profit it is to be supposed, for about three farthings per mile, loading and unloading the cargoes. That tons of human beings, loading and unloading themselves, can be carried much cheaper is self-evident. The actual cost of running a train carrying from 250 to 350 tons, and running at a speed of from 25 to 30 miles per hour, is not more than 6*d*. per mile—about 3*d*. for coals, and another 3*d*. for wages of engine-men and guards. A proof that it pays, even under the terribly wasteful management of our private companies, to charge low prices, is offered by the existence of the so-called "excursions"—somewhat dangerous comets in the planetary circle of rolling engines, and which might with great advantage be discontinued in favour of cheap ordinary trains.

2. The thorough suppression, as far as possible, of what are called "accidents." Mismanagement is the cause of nearly all of them. The vast number of lives lost annually in our present system of railway working is caused by what can be described only as reckless slaughter. Railway servants comprise the immense majority of the killed, for the simple reason, that

Railway accidents.

companies, being entirely formed and maintained on the basis of self-interest, and striving chiefly to divide large dividends, are as careless of the lives of those in their service as they are of the interests of the nation at large. In the single year 1878, the number of persons killed on the railways of the United Kingdom was 404, while the wounded numbered 1397. Of this total, 189 killed and 863 wounded were railway servants. Contrast this with France, on the railways of which—under State control, be it remembered—not more than five persons, passengers and servants together, were killed per annum on the average of the last five years. It is "manslaughter," clearly. What adds to the cruelty of this slaughter is that while the representatives of the killed passengers can demand "blood-money," the widows and children which the sacrificed railway servants—mostly men in the flower of age, the very pick of the population — leave behind them, have not even a claim to compensation. The wisdom of our legislature, in which the "railway interest" already referred to is so powerfully represented, has ordained it thus. Like the gladiators in the Roman arena, our stalwart railway men are mowed to the ground as if in sport, and may exclaim, like them, addressing their masters, "*Ave Cæsar Imperator morituri te salutant!*"

Railway Post Offices.

3. A greatly improved system of postal

services. If all our railways were under State control, like the postal and telegraph departments, every station could easily be turned also into a post office, when every train, without exception, could be accompanied by a travelling postal carriage for the sorting of letters as well as of parcels. In every town and village throughout the kingdom there would thus be as many despatches and as many deliveries of letters as there are stations and trains. It seems scarcely necessary to dwell upon the importance of this simultaneous increase of circulation of letters with that of travellers and of merchandise carried by railway. The progress of internal trade and the movement of population thus originated would probably not be less than that produced by the introduction of the railways themselves, when superseding the old stage coaches. Now millions travel against thousands in former times, while many hundreds of millions of letters are conveyed annually in mail-bags between the three corners of the kingdom. With still greater facilities of circulation, the communication between the thirty-four million inhabitants of the United Kingdom might easily be trebled and quadrupled. School boards will help in the matter. It was a wise remark of Richard Cobden that "letters make trade and trade makes letters."

4. The acquisition of the railways by the State, with consequent lowering of rates and

Equalization in value of landed property.

fares, would tend to equalize the value of landed property all over the kingdom. At present, a house with garden in Hampshire will bring but a fraction of the rent a similar one will at Kensington. The difference of rent usually can be measured by the amount of railway fare. It is very much the same with the price of goods, especially of articles of rapid consumption. A basket of fruit may not be worth more than one shilling at Appleham, yet fetch five shillings at Covent Garden, simply because the cost of transport between Appleham and Covent Garden amounts to four shillings. Reduce it to one-fourth and the basket would be sold for two shillings. With cheap transport the price of all commodities, food in particular, would naturally sink enormously. It is simply incalculable what the increase in value of landed property, removed from large centres of population, would be if railways were under national management, organized like the Post Office. The thought has often occurred to the writer of this paper that if our great landed proprietors knew their own interests they would have long ago striven, and used all their powerful influence, to bring about the purchase of railways by the State. As it is, railways have doubled the value of many an estate, and they would quintuple it to a certainty if our great iron highroads ceased to be matters of private speculation, and were managed in the interest of the nation.

The enumeration of the advantages to be derived from the purchase of our railways by the State by no means stops at the four chief points here indicated. Numerous others, beneficial to the nation, might be mentioned, such as, for example, the training of the army of railway servants as a militia for the defence of the country. It is an army of upwards of a quarter of a million of men, the whole in splendid *physique*, the very pick and flower of the population, inasmuch as the standards of strength and of health for the railway are much higher than those for the army, and a fair amount of education besides is insisted upon. However, these and other matters may well be left aside for the moment, the great object of this paper being to discuss the leading principles upon which it would be advisable to urge the early transfer of our railways from their present private ownership to the Government and the nation.

Proposed System of Purchase of Railways.

How could this transfer be effected ? This is the great question at the bottom of all, supposing the national advantages be admitted, as they scarcely can fail to be. At the first glance it seems a stupendous matter to deal with, an immense amount of capital being involved in the transaction ; still, if carefully considered, the difficulties in the way will be found really not

System of purchase of railways.

very great. The purchase of our railways by the State will be but a repetition, though on a greatly larger scale, of the purchase of telegraphs by the Government, and might be effected in much the same manner. It would be even easier to acquire the railways than it has been to buy the telegraphs, as there is already an Act of Parliament in existence— 7 and 8 Vict., cap. 85, dated 9th August, 1844 —which gives " powers of State to purchase railways," under conditions clearly specified. When this Act was passed, the whole of the railways of the kingdom might have been bought for something less than 200 millions sterling, whereas at present the cost will be about 700 millions. If waiting a few years longer, the bill of purchase may come to be a round thousand millions—a bill which, whatever may be said to the contrary, must be settled some day. All the nations of Europe, without exception, are settling their bills, and we must do the same in the end. To all who study the question seriously, with regard to the whole of its bearings, there can be no doubt that ultimately the new highways of all nations must become national property.

Present state of our railway system.

To put the whole question as to the present state of our railway system and its purchase by the nation in the smallest possible compass, the following table may be of service. It is taken from the official " General Report" upon railways issued by the Board of Trade, the dates as to mileage, total paid-up capital, ordinary capital, &c., referring to the 31st December, and the receipts, expenditure, percentages of earnings and dividends to each of the years 1877 and 1878 :—

Railways of the United Kingdom.	1877.	1878.
Total mileage	17,077	17,333
	£	£
Total paid-up capital	674,059,048	698,545,154
Capital per mile open	39,472	40,301
Ordinary capital, shares and stocks	265,041,233	265,675,340
Receipts :—		
From Passengers	26,534,110	26,889,614
„ Goods	34,109,947	33,564,761
Miscellaneous	2,329,271	2,408,299
Total receipts	62,973,328	62,862,674
Working Expenditure	33,857,978	33,189,368
Net earnings	29,115,350	29,673,306
	d.	d.
Receipts per train-mile from passenger and goods traffic	66·19	65·25
Expenditure per train-mile ..	35·82	34·69
Net earnings per train-mile	30·37	30·56
	Per cent.	Per cent.
Net earnings on capital ..	4·32	4·25
Dividend paid on ordinary capital	4·51	4·32

This is the picture of our railways *ab ovo* and in " a nutshell." We have 17,333 miles of railway, constructed at a cost of close upon 700 millions sterling, the annual revenue of which is a little under 63 millions, with a working expenditure of about 33½ millions, giving net earnings of 29½ millions. This produces net earnings and dividends of from 4¼ to 4½ per cent. on the total investment, as well as the ordinary capital, represented by shares and stocks. The 700 millions of paid-up capital, redeemed by the State, could, with the greatest facility, be converted into a public railway debt at 3½ per cent. interest, giving an immediate profit of about 1 per cent. interest to the nation. In reality, if the redemption be carried out promptly, the direct gain of interest would be much more by the vast reduction of working expenditure which would come in the wake of State management.

Dividends of our railways.

During each of the six years from 1873 to 1878 the rate of dividends paid on the ordinary capital, the guaranteed and preferential, the loans and debenture stock, and the total paid-up capital, shares and loans, was as follows, according to official returns :—

Years.	Ordinary Capital.		Guaranteed and Preferential Capital.	
	Amount.	Rate.	Amount.	Rate.
	£		£	
1873	12,199,274	4·99	8,429,611	4·48
1874	11,170,367	4·49	9,074,891	4·52
1875	12,018,009	4·72	9,634,276	4·54
1876	11,839,853	4·52	10,259,719	4·48
1877	11,948,594	4·51	10,604,901	4·47
1878	11,477,824	4·32	11,343,880	4·39

Years.	Loans and Debenture Stock.		Total Paid-up Capital.	
	Amount.	Rate.	Amount.	Rate.
	£		£	
1873	6,676,555	4·29	27,305,440	4·64
1874	6,870,370	4·28	27,115,628	4·45
1875	6,957,716	4·26	28,610,001	4·54
1876	7,124,511	4·26	29,224,083	4·44
1877	7,301,920	4·25	29,855,415	4·43
1878	7,366,223	4·23	30,187,927	4·32

In the "General Report" of the Board of Trade upon railways, issued in 1879, it is shown with great minuteness what differing rates of dividends and interest were paid upon the total capital in the year 1878. The result as regards the ordinary capital of all the railways is summarized as follows :— *(Divisions of capital and dividends.)*

38	millions of capital received	no dividend.
$5\frac{1}{2}$	,, ,, ,,	not more than 1 per cent.
$14\frac{1}{2}$	,, ,, ,,	1 to 2 per cent.
$10\frac{1}{2}$	,, ,, ,,	2 to 3 ,,
$26\frac{1}{2}$	,, ,, ,,	3 to 4 ,,
$27\frac{1}{2}$	,, ,, ,,	4 to 5 ,,
$74\frac{3}{4}$	,, ,, ,,	5 to 6 ,,
62	,, ,, ,,	6 to 7 ,,
$3\frac{1}{4}$	,, ,, ,,	7 to 8 ,,
$1\frac{3}{4}$	,, ,, ,,	8 to 10 ,,

By the terms of the Act of Parliament of 1844, previously referred to, the "Lords Commissioners of Her Majesty's Treasury" are empowered to purchase, "at the expiration of the term of twenty-one years" from that date, "any railway, with all its hereditaments, stock, and appurtenances, in the name and on behalf of *(Act of Parliament for purchase of railways.)*

Her Majesty, upon giving to the company three calendar months' notice in writing of their intention, and upon payment of a sum equal to twenty-five years' purchase of the annual divisible profits, estimated on the average of the three then next preceding years." In order to deal fairly and liberally with railway proprietors getting small dividends, or none at all, it is further provided that " if the average rate of profits for the three years shall be less than the rate of 10*l.* in the 100*l.*, it shall be lawful for the company, if they shall be of opinion that the said rate of twenty-five years' purchase of the said average profits is an inadequate rate of purchase of such railway, reference being had to the prospects thereof, to require that it shall be left to arbitration, in case of difference, to determine what, if any, additional amount of purchase-money shall be paid to the company." It is certain that there would be rejoicing in the camp of the railway shareholders who own the 38 millions of capital which now receive no dividends, as well as the additional owners of some 30 millions which only get from 1 to 3 per cent., if the " Lords Commissioners of Her Majesty's Treasury " would bring the Act of 1844 into operation. But the nation still more than those shareholders would have reason to be grateful.

The saving in expenditure which might be d by an efficient State management of our railways, would be a saving to the nation, and allow not only the application of very low rates and fares for goods and passengers, but a vastly improved service. Under their present management the organization of the service, dictated more often by mean jealousy of the different companies to each other than by reasonable self-interest, is in a state approaching chaos. To get an idea of it, one has to visit only the terminal stations of three of our great railways near to each other, the London and North-Western, the Midland, and the Great Northern, at Euston, St. Pancras, and King's Cross. Every morning and every evening there rush forth from these stations express trains to Edinburgh, Glasgow, and the North of Scotland. These trains, magnificently equipped, run at the rate of about fifty miles an hour, and very seldom, except at certain seasons, are as much as half filled. It is certain that these wonderful express trains—kept going not for the benefit of the masses, but for that of a select class, including the one thousand railway directors of the United Kingdom—do not pay their working expenses ; and it is equally certain that the three trains combined into one could carry the whole of the passengers going by them, if at a somewhat lesser speed decidedly also at greatly reduced fares, and at much less risk to life and limb. But not only the wealthy companies north of the Thames indulge in these " express " luxuries, for the benefit only of a very restricted class, but the small companies south of the river think themselves entitled to imitate the example. Every morning and every evening the Chatham and Dover and the South-Eastern Companies dispatch express " mail " trains from London to Dover and back, starting and arriving at the same hours. In ninety-nine cases out of a hundred throughout the year these two trains are each less than one-half filled, and it is quite beyond doubt that one train morning and evening could carry at any time and any day all the passengers that wish to go to Dover by the " mail."

Wasteful railway expenditure.

The waste of resources thus occasioned will, it may be argued, fall on the shareholders of all these companies—even on such as those of the unfortunate London, Chatham, and Dover Company, who never receive dividends. But this is taking a narrow view of the matter. In reality, not the shareholders but the public must, in the end, pay for wastefulness and improvidence in railway management. If the companies lose money by running express trains, designed entirely for the benefit of the " upper ten," and kept up " regardless of expense," the loss must be recouped by placing " the million " under contribution, taxing them in the shape of exorbitantly high fares. This is systematically done by all our railway companies.

To sum up the arguments adduced and the proposals made in this paper, a few words may suffice. Our modern iron roads have taken the place of the old "Queen's highway," and as such they ought to be public property, managed for the benefit and in the interest of the nation. Instead of a thousand directors and scores of general managers, with allowances equal to those of cabinet ministers, there should be one central government of all the lines, with the service so arranged as to meet the utmost public convenience. As a rule there need be few trains running at a higher speed than about thirty miles an hour; there need be no more than two classes of carriages. To prevent so-called "accidents," entirely preventable, goods trains should, as far as possible, never run on the same lines as passenger trains. This could be very easily arranged if the railways were national property, inasmuch as one or more of the competing lines now connecting all the great centres of population could, for through traffic, be reserved entirely for the carriage of goods, leaving the other for passengers. The fares for passengers, calculated on the lowest paying rate for their transport, might ultimately be made uniform, or nearly so; but provisionally there might be adopted a system of "zones," before sketched out, under which most of the absurdities of the present system of high charges would disappear.